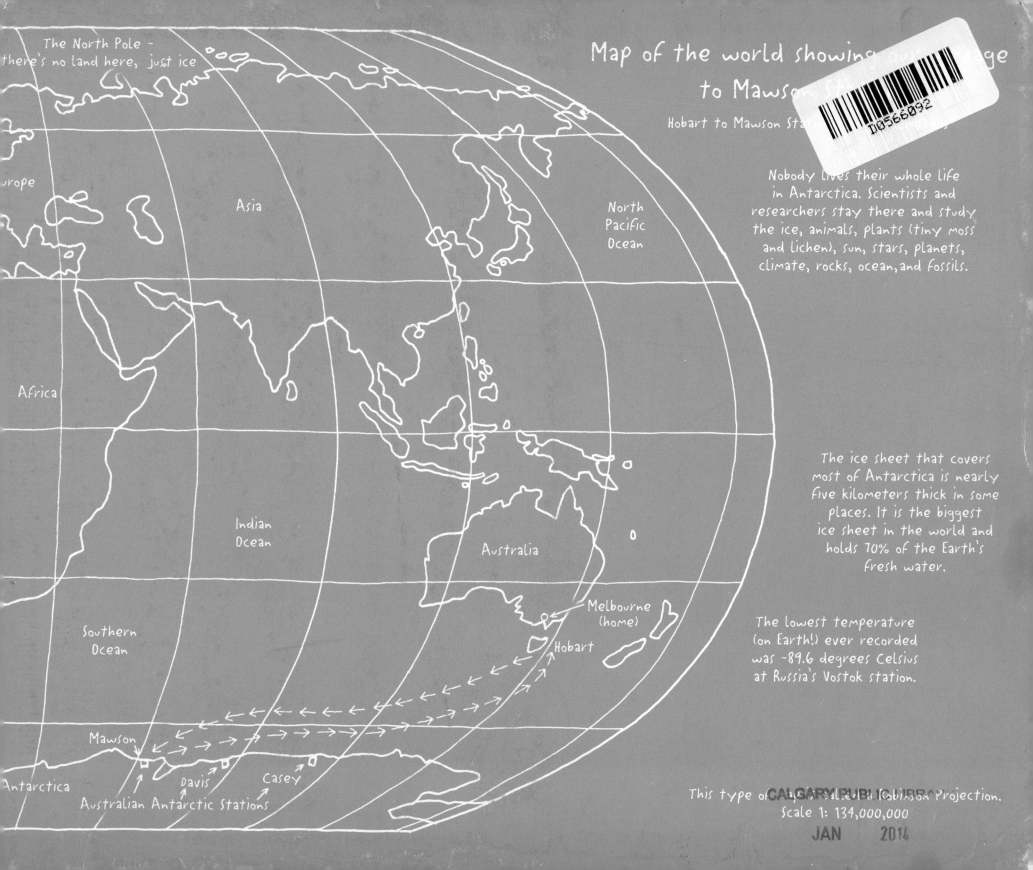

The North Pole –
there's no land here, just ice

Europe

Asia

North
Pacific
Ocean

Africa

Indian
Ocean

Australia

Melbourne
(home)

Southern
Ocean

Hobart

Mawson

Davis

Casey

Antarctica

Australian Antarctic Stations

Map of the world showing our voyage to Mawson Station

Hobart to Mawson Station

Nobody lives their whole life in Antarctica. Scientists and researchers stay there and study the ice, animals, plants (tiny moss and lichen), sun, stars, planets, climate, rocks, ocean, and fossils.

The ice sheet that covers most of Antarctica is nearly five kilometers thick in some places. It is the biggest ice sheet in the world and holds 70% of the Earth's fresh water.

The lowest temperature (on Earth!) ever recorded was -89.6 degrees Celsius at Russia's Vostok station.

This type of map is called a Robinson Projection.
Scale 1: 134,000,000

For Coral Tulloch

In 2005 I traveled to Mawson Station as an Australian Antarctic Arts Fellow aboard the *Aurora Australis*. Every day
of the six-week voyage I sent an email to schools and families around the world, describing my experiences. Children
drew their responses to my stories and sent copies of their work to me. I used these drawings to make an exhibition
called Kids Antarctic Art. The exhibition has toured Australia and overseas for years now and profits from prints
sold go the Royal Children's Hospital in Melbourne. Many of the pictures in Sophie Scott's diary are from the
exhibition so a proportional percentage of the book's royalties will go to the Royal Children's Hospital, too.

Thanks to the Australian Antarctic Division, crew and fellow passengers from my 2005 voyage, and the kids, parents,
and teachers who supported the project. Thanks also to Simon Estella and Shaun Deshommes from P&O Australia,
Mike Craven, Dr. Ben Maddison, Coral Tulloch, Warwick Barnes for his photographs, Jade McKenna for initial design
and collation, the team at Penguin, and the team at home.

SOPHIE SCOTT GOES SOUTH

ALISON LESTER

Houghton Mifflin Books for Children
Houghton Mifflin Harcourt
Boston New York 2013

Mum

Alfie

Woohoo! I'm going to Antarctica!

That's right, me, Sophie Scott.

I'm nine years old and I'm going to Antarctica with my dad.

He's the captain of the *Aurora Australis*. It's an icebreaker— a ship that can go through ice. We're delivering people and supplies to Mawson Station. We'll be the last visitors there before winter comes and the ocean freezes.

We'll be at sea for about a month. It will take nearly two weeks to get there, then after a week at Mawson it will be time to come home.

I'll see icebergs, penguins, seals, and whales. Dad says there might even be blizzards.

I can't wait!

Dad

me

Things I will see in Antarctica

No polar bears! They're only in the Arctic.

Day 1

Mum was being brave when she hugged me goodbye at the airport, but I could see tears in her eyes. Alfie was sad too, so I promised to bring him back some Antarctic ice. When our plane was arriving in Hobart I could see the *Aurora Australis* in the harbor. She looked tiny from the air, but when I stood beside her (Dad says ships are always girls) I could see she was enormous, as long as a football field and five stories high.

Dad has these stamps in his desk on the bridge.

Dad carried my bags to our cabin and I unpacked my things. My bunk has a little curtain I can pull across. There's a reading light just above my pillow and it feels like a treehouse. It's nice knowing Dad will be just on the other side of the cabin.

I climbed up to the top deck and watched as passengers lugged bags up the gangway, and a big crane swung a net full of cargo onto the ship.

When everything was packed, Dad blew the horn and the ship moved slowly away from the dock. We threw brightly colored streamers to the people waving and held on until the streamers snapped and the water between us got wider and wider.

As we left Hobart, a big moon reflected on the water and lights twinkled along the hills. I felt like an astronaut, heading into outer space, a bit scared, but very excited.

This is the
Aurora Australis

anchors

  FIRE HOSE

 AURORA AUSTRALIS HOBART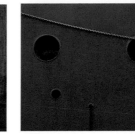

switches

lifeboat

winch

gangway

   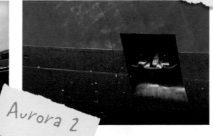 

life ring

Aurora 2

 LIFEBUOY     AURORA AUSTRALIS

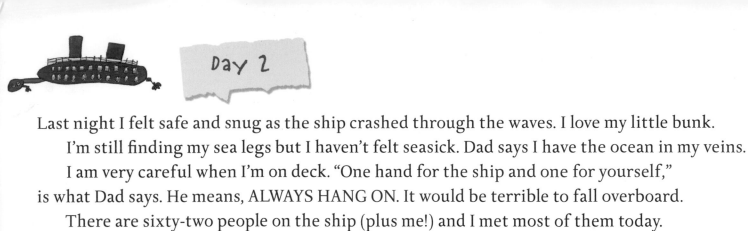

Last night I felt safe and snug as the ship crashed through the waves. I love my little bunk.

I'm still finding my sea legs but I haven't felt seasick. Dad says I have the ocean in my veins.

I am very careful when I'm on deck. "One hand for the ship and one for yourself," is what Dad says. He means, ALWAYS HANG ON. It would be terrible to fall overboard.

There are sixty-two people on the ship (plus me!) and I met most of them today. Twenty-three are crew members and the rest are the Mawson resupply expedition. They are:

- the voyage leader and his deputy
- sixteen people going to stay at Mawson for a year
- twelve visiting scientists
- six people to drive boats
- two crane operators
- one artist (Mum's friend Sarah).

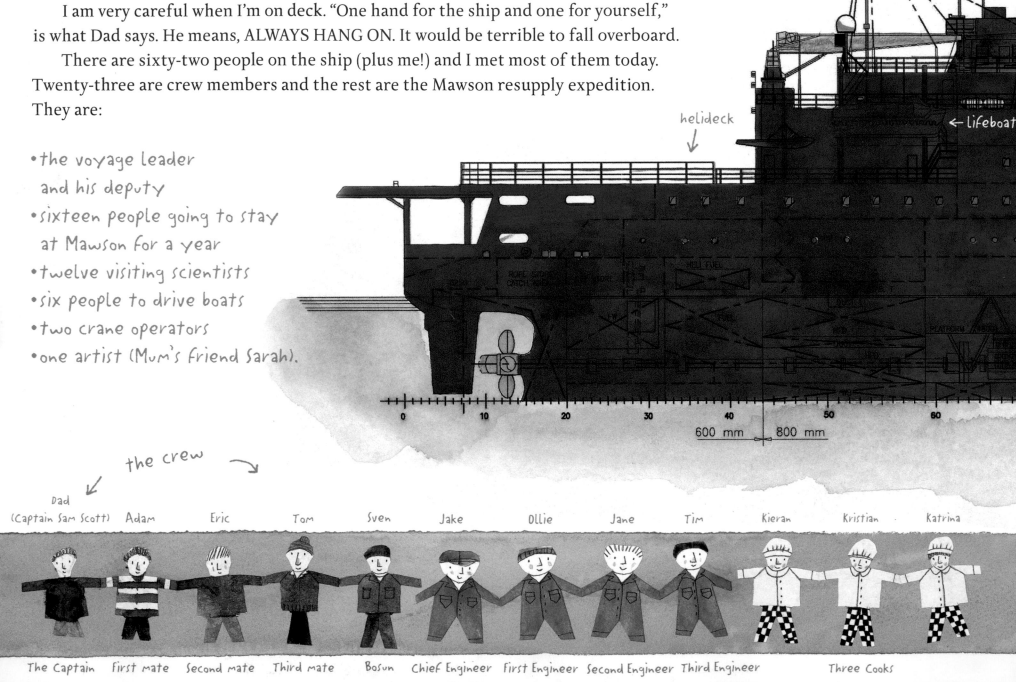

helideck

←Lifeboat

600 mm   800 mm

the crew

Dad
(Captain Sam Scott)   Adam   Eric   Tom   Sven   Jake   Ollie   Jane   Tim   Kieran   Kristian   Katrina

The Captain   First mate   Second mate   Third mate   Bosun   Chief Engineer   First Engineer   Second Engineer   Third Engineer   Three Cooks

Some things on the ship have special names. My bunk is called a berth, the window is a porthole, the kitchen is the galley, and the dining room is the mess. I made a new friend today, Georgie, who is going to Mawson for a year to study penguins. She taught me a dance called the Penguin Strut.

This morning we put on our life jackets and all went to the helideck for a muster where we learned about safety and rescue. We climbed into the big orange lifeboats hanging off the side of the ship. Each one fits seventy people and the toilet is a bucket. The food is stale sea biscuits.

I hope we don't ever have to use the lifeboats. Dad says I shouldn't worry. He's been to Antarctica lots of times and never been shipwrecked.

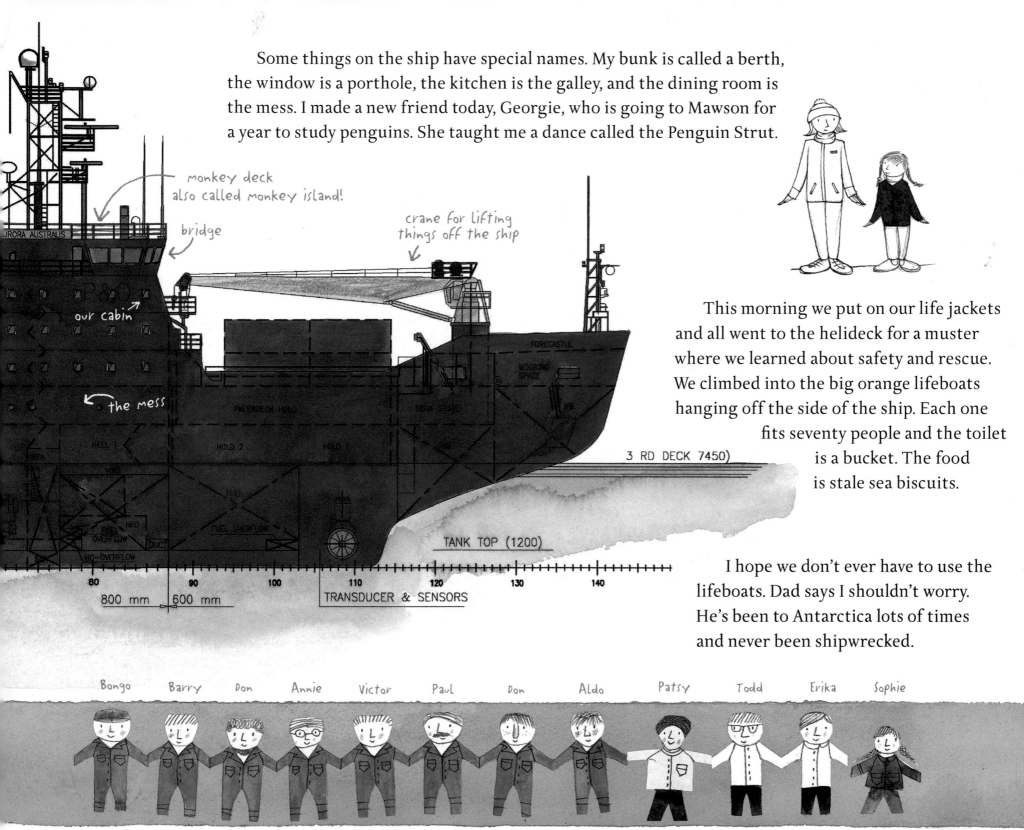

monkey deck
also called monkey island!

bridge

crane for lifting
things off the ship

AURORA AUSTRALIS

P&O

our cabin

the mess

FORECASTLE

MOORING
SPACE

HEEL 1

HOLD 2

HOLD 1

DECK STORE

3 RD DECK 7450)

FUEL

FUEL OVERFLOW

FUEL OVERFLOW

HO OVERFLOW

DUCT

TANK TOP (1200)

80   90   100   110   120   130   140

800 mm | 600 mm

TRANSDUCER & SENSORS

Bongo   Barry   Don   Annie   Victor   Paul   Don   Aldo   Patsy   Todd   Erika   Sophie

Eight able-bodied seamen   Chief Steward   Two Stewards   and me

Day 5

I've missed a couple of days in my diary because the sea has been so rough. Last night the ship was rocking and rolling like crazy. Anything that's not tied down goes flying and I have to hold on all the time. Sometimes a wave bashes the ship so hard that it feels as though we've hit a rock. The dining room portholes go underwater every time the ship does a big roll. It's like we're eating inside a washing machine. Hardly anyone came to breakfast this morning because lots of people are seasick.

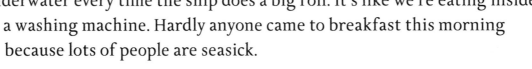

    Mum's friend Sarah has given me a desk in her studio where I can draw and paint. It's a tiny cabin with no windows. Sarah says that being in this room is like being in the belly of a whale because the pipes in the walls moan and groan, like a rumbling tummy. I'm not allowed to go on deck by myself when the sea is this rough, but this afternoon Dad let me go with Sarah to take some photos.

    The wind was so strong and cold I could hardly breathe. The ship rolled beneath us like a bucking horse and we watched an albatross sweep over the waves.

Day 7

When I looked out my porthole this morning there were two big icebergs on the horizon! My first icebergs!

Dad steered the ship close to one and it was as big as a fifteen-story building. It looked like a giant crouching lion.

We also passed a jade iceberg, and one with a big black stripe. The stripe was rock that had been picked up by the ice when it was part of a glacier grinding slowly over Antarctica.

snow falls and compresses into ice

chunks of ice break off and become icebergs

ice shelf

→ glacier moves slowly to coast then over ocean

ocean

Antarctic continent

cross-section showing how an iceberg is formed

I was toasty today in my special polar clothes. First I put on a thermal top and long johns, thick woolen socks, neck warmer, polar-fleece top and pants, freezer suit, insulated snow boots, mittens, beanie, sunglasses, and finally a big Gore-Tex jacket. I looked like a Teletubby.

As we head toward Antarctica it feels as though we are entering an icy kingdom and the icebergs are guarding it.

I saw heaps of icebergs today and gave them all names.
↓

Furry Cat	Big Shoe	The Tooth	Money Box	Ice Hut	Archway	Dog	Big Dipper	Lion

ICEBERGS

I'd love to paddle a canoe through here. ↑

↓ tabular bergs ↑

berg with a stripe ←

jade berg ←

First berg in the shape of a lion ↙

Brrrrr! I'm so cold I can hardly type. Last night there was a wild blizzard, and I couldn't sleep. I was sliding up and down in my bed like a yoyo. This morning the decks were covered with ice and snow, and it was too dangerous to go outside.

After lunch the storm died down and the ship had to go slowly because the sea was covered with broken-up ice.

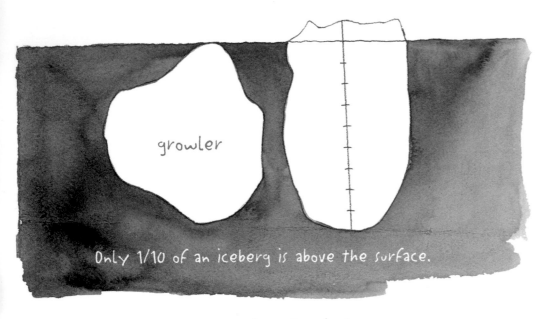

growler

Only 1/10 of an iceberg is above the surface.

Cross-section of an iceberg

There were loud BONGS as icebergs just below the surface bashed into the ship's hull. Adam, the first mate, told me these icebergs are called growlers.

I loved looking at the ice cracking as the *Aurora* pushed through it, and while I was watching, A SEAL POKED ITS HEAD THROUGH THE ICE!

It looked right at me and I waved and shouted, "Hello seal!," then it was gone.

Georgie said it was a crab-eater seal. They don't eat crabs, they eat krill. Maybe they should be called krill-eater seals.

I saw my first penguins too—six Adelies standing on an ice floe. They looked like tiny waiters in dinner suits.

The sun didn't set until 10:30, and by the time I came inside, my toes and fingers were frozen.

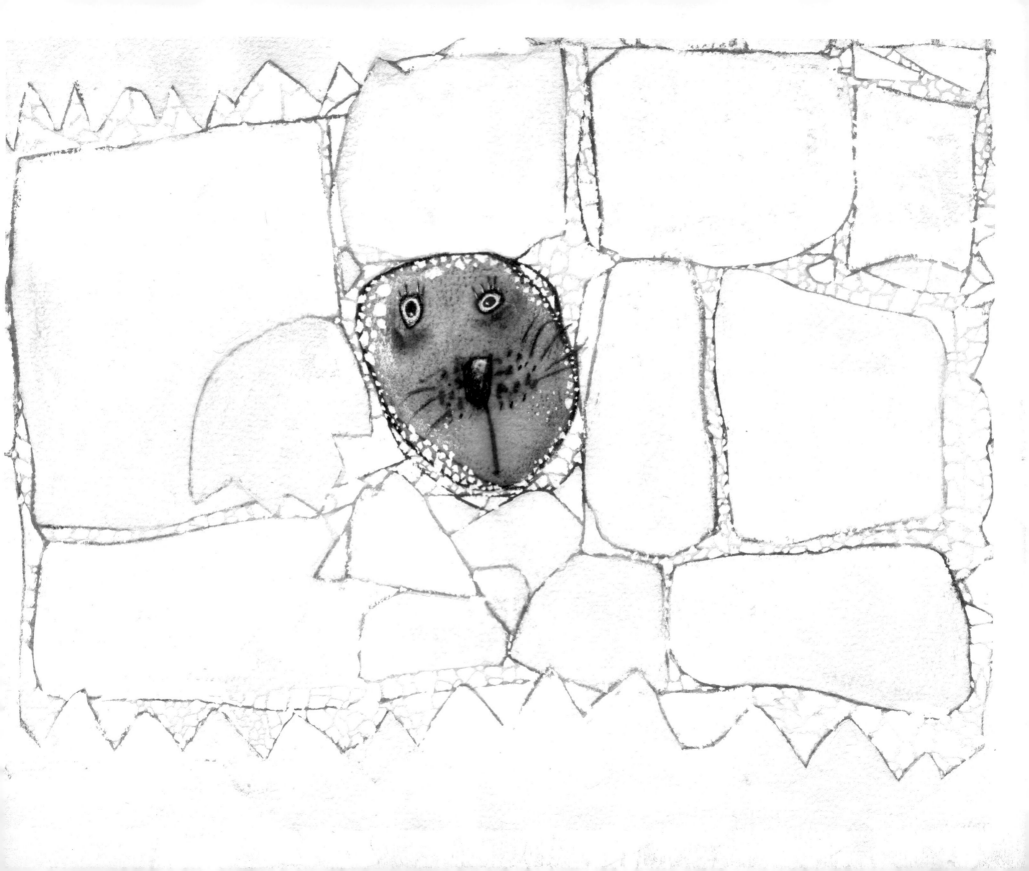

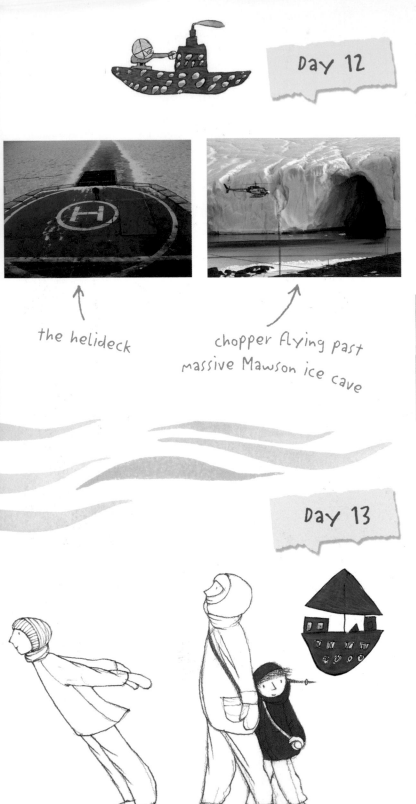

the helideck

chopper flying past
massive Mawson ice cave

Dad thought we would be at Mawson Station this morning, but the sea ice is too thick for us to go any closer. He's worried we'll get stuck if we keep going, so the ship has stopped. We can see the mountain peaks behind Mawson and it's driving everybody crazy that we are so close but we still can't get there.

I helped sweep the ice and snow off the helideck so the helicopters can take the visiting scientists ashore. They only have a week to do their work, so they need to start straight away. Georgie went on the helicopter, but Sarah is still on the ship with me. We're keeping our fingers crossed that the ice will clear.

lines on the sea show it's really windy

big cracks in the ice

frozen waves

Day 13

Hooray! Last night the wind blew so hard it shifted the sea ice, clearing the way for the ship to get to Mawson. I stood on the Monkey Deck as we went in and the wind was like a freezing hurricane. I couldn't hold my camera steady and I couldn't stand up unless I was sheltering behind someone.

Dad steered the ship into tiny Horseshoe Harbor and parked her like a car. People from Mawson sped out to the ship in rubber boats. They picked up the mooring ropes and took them back to bollards on the rocky shore. Soon the *Aurora Australis* was tied up safely. I felt very proud when I heard people saying what a great skipper Scotty was.

Day 14

This morning I was so excited about going ashore that I woke up too early and Dad made me go back to bed for a while. After breakfast we climbed down a rope ladder to a barge waiting below. It was scary trying to hang on, with the ship moving up and down.

When I stepped on land my smile was so big it felt like my face was going to crack. I was standing on Antarctica!

The ground was rough and rocky, with patches of snow. Thick ropes linked all the buildings and Sarah told me this is to stop you from getting lost in a blizzard.

We walked up to the Red Shed, the big building that the Mawson people live in. As soon as I got inside I started to feel sick and dizzy. It felt as if the building was heaving like a ship: up, down, up, down. I didn't feel seasick on the ship, but I was seasick on land!

The station leader, Janie, said this happens to lots of people. She welcomed everybody and told us the station rules, then we helped put away supplies. There were huge boxes of toothpaste, toilet paper, soap, and shampoo, and massive amounts of food, like 5400 eggs and 165 tubs of ice cream!

a Weddell seal . . .

. . . scratching his nose

Later, Georgie took me for a walk and we watched a Weddell seal scratching his whiskers with a flipper. He was groaning and moaning, and I think he had eaten too many fish.

It was good to get back to the ship tonight and show Dad my photos. Katrina brought me dinner in bed because I was so tired.

Weddell seals under the ice

When we went ashore this morning, Sarah and I explored around the station. We had lunch in the Red Shed, then Geoff, the station doctor, took us for a drive up to the plateau. We went in a Hägglund, which is a kind of snowmobile. It was very noisy and bumpy.

As we went up the hill, the Hägglund couldn't get a grip and kept slipping backwards towards the sea! I was thinking how bad it would be to crash into the freezing water when Geoff FINALLY gunned it to the top, and we all cheered.

Before we got out, we hooked spiky chains under our boots because the ice was as slippery as glass. I took some photos, but we didn't stay for long because it was so cold. As we bumped back to the station, the sky went dark and hail started bashing against the windshield. When we got out of the Hägglund it was snowing so heavily we could hardly see. Sarah and I held on to the ropes between the buildings and finally got to the Red Shed.

When Janie called Dad on the radio he told us we would have to stay ashore. The weather was too wild for us to go back to the ship.

It was a BLIZZARD! I was stranded in Antarctica!

Georgie put mattresses on the floor of her room for Sarah and me, and we were like little mice, snuggled up together. Just before I went to sleep, Georgie played me a recording of a Weddell seal singing under the ice and its lovely song stayed in my head all night.

Uh oh!

Mawson Station

communications shed

This is called an apple hut.

Hägglund

wind turbine

ice!

snow!

my feet!

Antarctic caravan
I took this photo from the Red Shed.

the Red Shed

an Antarctic trailer

ship with crane up

quad bikes

Day 16

This morning the wind was howling and the walls of the Red Shed shook as though a monster was trying to get in. It was way too dangerous to go outside.

Fourteen people from the ship were stranded ashore and we all helped with jobs. I dried dishes and helped Sarah mop the floor.

Everybody was kind to me, but I felt lonely and worried about Dad. I watched the ship swinging from side to side, and it looked as though the ropes would break, for sure.

In the afternoon the blizzard got so strong that we couldn't even see the *Aurora*.

It was a white-out.

11 am

12:30 pm

1:45 pm

3 pm

Georgie and Sarah played Polar Scrabble with me, and I think they let me win. After lunch, Janie gave me the phone so I could talk to Mum and Alfie. While Mum was talking I could hear the magpies singing outside our house.

By dinnertime, the blizzard had died down. It was still too dangerous to go back to the ship, but we were allowed to go outside. When Georgie and I went walking we had to hold on to each other to keep from being blown over. We saw an Adelie penguin, completely covered in ice. Georgie said it wouldn't feel cold because penguin feathers are good insulation.

Sarah made this picture of an emperor penguin. I helped do the dots.

Last night Sarah and Georgie woke me up to show me a surprise. They helped me get dressed, we went outside, and they pointed up. A band of light stretched across the sky, shimmering and dancing in front of the stars. It began over the sea and swooped above us in a wide stripe of neon green. It was as though a ghost had zoomed across the sky then disappeared with a flick of its tail.

It was an aurora. They're caused when particles from the sun crash into the earth's atmosphere above the poles. In the Arctic it's called *aurora borealis*. In Antarctica its name is *aurora australis*, the same as our ship.

I woke up to a sunny day today and a nice surprise because Dad arrived while I was having breakfast. It was great to see him and he hugged me until I had to yell for a breath.

I took him to see the penguins and we had a go on the climbing wall. Dad was hopeless, but I could climb like a spider. After that, we went back to the ship.

We have two more days at Mawson, and when we leave, there will be no more visitors for seven months. Only sixteen people will stay here for winter. That's when Georgie will ride her quad bike over the sea ice to Auster Rookery. She'll live on nearby Macey Island in a tiny red apple hut and study the emperor penguins. There are more than 20,000 penguins there. That's a lot of penguins.

Mike — station leader
Helen — new doctor
Rod — chef
Ernie, Karl — two plumbers
Alan, Suzanne — two meteorologists
Jahzeel, Maureen — two communications experts
Cliff, Ian — two mechanics
Sally — one carpenter
Daphne, Fritz — two electricians
Eric — electrical engineer
Georg — biologist

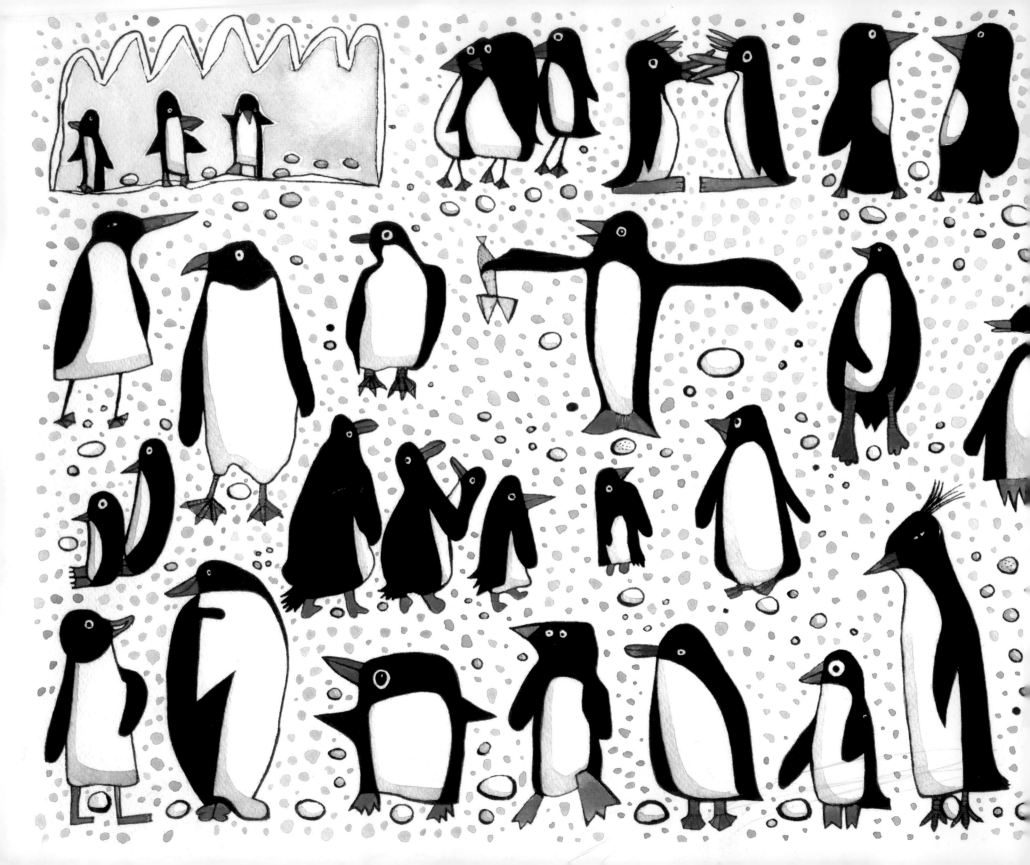

BYE BYE GEORGIE

Goodbye, Mawson!

This morning the helicopters flew out to the ship. We are taking them home with us. I watched the engineers unscrew the rotor blades and stow them in a big box. Then they pushed the choppers into the hangar and tied them down.

After lunch I heard the ship's hooter and raced up on deck to wave to Georgie. Everybody staying at Mawson came down to Horseshoe Harbor to say farewell to us. They let off pink flares that drifted down through the snowy sky.

The sea was freezing into little pancakes of ice and Dad was anxious to get going. If we weren't quick, we'd be stuck at Mawson for the winter!

We crashed through the ice all afternoon. Some bits were so big that the ship tilted as she slid over them.

All the people who have been at Mawson are excited to be going home. The visiting scientists have done their work, and I think Dad and the crew are happy that we didn't get stuck.

After dinner we had a King Neptune ceremony to celebrate crossing the Antarctic Circle. We should have had it on the way down, but the weather was too rough. Adam was dressed up as King Neptune and Dad was a mermaid.

We had to kiss a dead fish.

YUCK!

Antarctic
Colors

Everyone told me
Antarctica would be white,
but look at this!

Day 22

The ice has been so thick it's taken us three days to get this far. This morning at sunrise we saw some killer whales beside the ship. Their shiny black bodies stood out against the golden sea. Some were putting their heads right out of the water as we went past. This is called spy-hopping.

After lunch Sarah showed me photos from her polar trips and told me about some of the famous Antarctic explorers.

This is Roald Amundsen from Norway, who was first to the South Pole in 1911.

This is Sir Ernest Shackleton. He was from Ireland. In 1909 he nearly made it to the South Pole, but had to turn back when he ran out of food. Afterwards he said to his wife, "A live donkey is better than a dead lion, isn't it?" Shackleton is famous for getting all his men home safely after his ship the Endurance was crushed by ice in 1914.

Sir Robert Scott (same name as me!) was also called Scott of the Antarctic. He was English. He tried to be first to the South Pole, but Amundsen beat him by a month. He and his men starved to death on their way back.

And this is Sir Douglas Mawson from Australia who explored Antarctica. In 1912 he made it through terrible blizzards after both his companions died. This time of Antarctic history is called the Heroic Age because the explorers were so brave.

Scott's hut at Cape Evans

Amundsen's hut

Mawson's hut at Commonwealth Bay

The Endurance being crushed

The stove that kept Shackleton's hut warm

Day 25

We've been out of the ice for two days now. This morning the ship stopped to pick up an underwater microphone called an acoustic recording package. The scientists on the ship left it here a year ago to record the ocean noises.

Today the technicians floated it to the surface. Whale experts back home will listen and find out what the whales have been saying.

After lunch it was sunny, even though it was still minus four degrees. Sarah and I took photos of the cooks pretending to sunbake in front of an iceberg.

That was our last iceberg. I felt sad that we wouldn't see any more. When we were in the ice it seemed they would last forever.

It was Dad's birthday today and I got to carry out the cake on a big silver tray.

Tonight the sun set over confused seas. I love that name, it sounds as if the sea can't figure something out, but it really means there are waves coming from all directions.

Only four days until we get home. I'm going to miss my little bunk that rocks me to sleep every night.

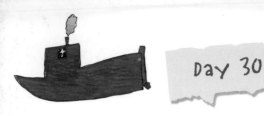

 Day 30

When I woke up this morning the ship wasn't moving and when I looked out my porthole, there was Hobart!

We were tied up to the dock.

After breakfast we all swapped email addresses and said goodbye. Sarah gave me a beautiful painting of whales and icebergs to take home to Mum. Then everybody walked down the gangway with their bags. The ship felt still and quiet when they were gone.

I packed up my things, peeled my pictures off the wall, then lay on my bunk and waited for Dad. Soon he came.

"Come on, Sophie of the Antarctic," he said. "Let's go home."

And so we did.

Alfie's ice

Glossary

ALBATROSS – a large oceanic bird

ANTARCTICA – the continent that surrounds the South Pole

ANTARCTIC CIRCLE – a parallel of latitude, about 66 degrees, 33 minutes south. At midsummer the sun does not set south of here.

ANTARCTIC TREATY – a set of rules about the use of Antarctica

APPLE HUT – round, red, fiberglass, transportable field hut

AURORA – luminous light above the North and South Poles

BARGE – flat-bottomed boat used for loading and unloading goods

BIOLOGIST – somebody who studies living things

BOLLARD – short, strong post

CARGO – goods carried on a ship

EMPEROR PENGUIN – the largest penguin

FLARE – a device that gives off a colored light

FREEZER SUIT – insulated suit for extremely cold conditions

GANGWAY – temporary bridge between ship and shore

GLACIER – a river of ice, moving slowly toward the sea

GORE-TEX – waterproof material

HÄGGLUND – Swedish, diesel-powered, all-terrain vehicle

HANGAR – a building where aircraft are kept

HELI-DECK – place for a helicopter to land

ICEBREAKER – a ship designed to break its way through ice

ICE SHEET – extensive area of ice, usually over land

ICE SHELF – huge area of very thick floating ice, attached to land

INSULATION – stops the transfer of heat

KATABATIC WIND – a wind produced when cold dense air flows downwards

KILLER WHALE – not actually a whale; a black-and-white carnivorous marine mammal

KING NEPTUNE – Roman god of the sea

LONG JOHNS – long underwear

KRILL – tiny shrimps found in huge swarms in the Southern Ocean

MAWSON STATION – most westerly of Australia's Antarctic stations

MERMAID – an imaginary sea creature with a woman's body and a fish's tail

METEOROLOGIST – somebody who understands the atmosphere and weather

MONKEY DECK – small open deck above the bridge of a ship

MOORING ROPES – ropes that hold a ship to the shore

MUSTER – an assembly

NEON – gas used in some electric lights

NUNATAK – a mountain peak sticking up from an ice sheet. It means "lonely stone."

PANCAKE ICE – little floes of sea ice, the beginnings of pack ice

PACK ICE – a large area of (dense) sea ice blocks that move about with ocean currents and surface winds

PLATEAU – a flat area of high land

POLAR FLEECE – fabric designed for very cold conditions

POLAR FRONT – the area of the Southern Ocean where the cold Antarctic water meets the warmer subantarctic water

SEA ICE – any ice that is formed by the freezing of the sea

SOUTH POLE – the most southerly place on earth

WEDDELL SEAL – seal that spends most of its time under the ice, and sings and whistles

WINCH – a lifting or pulling device

WHITE-OUT – when the sun, shadows, and horizon can't be seen. Everything is white.

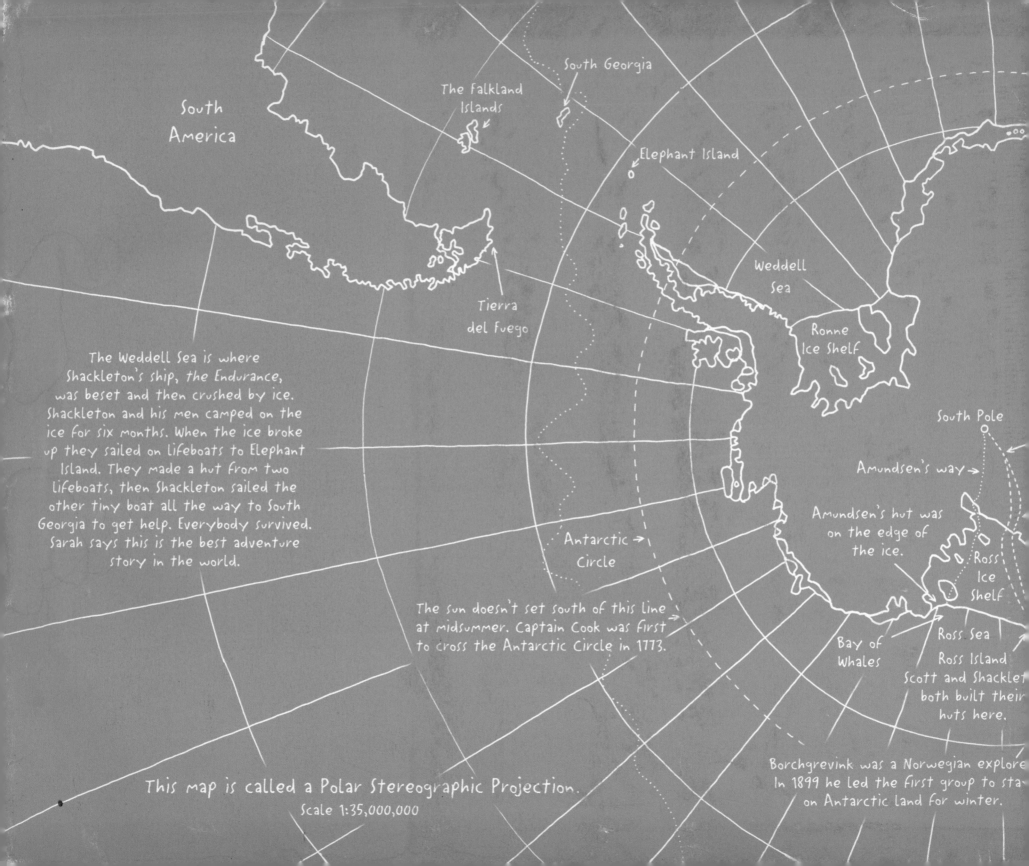

South
America

South Georgia

The Falkland
Islands

Elephant Island

Tierra
del Fuego

Weddell
Sea

Ronne
Ice Shelf

South Pole

Amundsen's way →

Amundsen's hut was
on the edge of
the ice.

Ross
Ice
Shelf

The Weddell Sea is where
Shackleton's ship, the Endurance,
was beset and then crushed by ice.
Shackleton and his men camped on the
ice for six months. When the ice broke
up they sailed on lifeboats to Elephant
Island. They made a hut from two
lifeboats, then Shackleton sailed the
other tiny boat all the way to South
Georgia to get help. Everybody survived.
Sarah says this is the best adventure
story in the world.

Antarctic →
Circle

The sun doesn't set south of this line
at midsummer. Captain Cook was first
to cross the Antarctic Circle in 1773.

Bay of
Whales

Ross Sea

Ross Island
Scott and Shacklet
both built their
huts here.

Borchgrevink was a Norwegian explore
In 1899 he led the first group to sta
on Antarctic land for winter.

This map is called a Polar Stereographic Projection.
Scale 1:35,000,000